Holy Spirit Workbook

Dr. Cheryl Salem

Scripture quotations taken from the Amplified® Bible (AMPC), Copyright © 1954, 1958, 1962, 1964, 1965, 1987 by The Lockman Foundation. Used by permission.

Holy Spirit Workbook

ISBN 9798801887340

Printed in United States of America

Copyright © 2022 by Salem Family Ministries

Salem Family Ministries

PO Box 1595

Cathedral City, CA 92235

www.salemfamilyministries.org

No part of this book may be reproduced or transmitted in any form or by any means, electronic or mechanical, including photocopying, recording, or by any information storage and retrieval system, without permission in writing from Salem Family Ministries.

Disclaimer: The views expressed in this book contain personal opinions and experiences throughout my life and time spent in God's presence. I express them as my opinion and view only and share them with you from my personal lifelong experience and from my heart. I am only communicating what has worked for me personally and what I have personally experienced with the Lord.

Table of Contents

Chapter One . . . . Who Is the Holy Spirit?

Chapter Two . . . . Where Does the Holy Spirit Live?

Chapter Three . . . . How Do I Receive the Holy Spirit?

Chapter Four . . . . What Is the Work of the Holy Spirit?

Chapter Five . . . . How Do I Yield to the Holy Spirit?

Chapter Six . . . . What Are the Gifts of the Holy Spirit?

Chapter Seven . . . . What Is the Fruit of the Holy Spirit?

Chapter Eight . . . . The Correlation Between the Fruit and the Gifts of the Holy Spirit

Chapter Nine . . . . Jesus' Relationship With the Holy Spirit

Chapter Ten . . . . The Nature of the Spirit of God Is Fire

Chapter Eleven . . . . Three Baptisms: Water, Holy Spirit, and Fire

Chapter Twelve . . . . The Holy Spirit Speaks and Sings Through You

Chapter Thirteen . . . . The Hierarchy of the Kingdom of God

Chapter Fourteen . . . . How To Be Led by the Holy Spirit

Chapter Fifteen . . . . The Seven-Fold Spirits of God

Chapter Sixteen . . . . Holy Spirit Is Our Witness in Heaven and on Earth

How To Use This Workbook

The Holy Spirit Workbook is designed to be a companion personal journal. As you walk through the pages of Holy Spirit, use the workbook to delve deeper in His presence in your own personal life and experience with our precious Holy Spirit. The Father gave us Jesus first as our Lord and Savior, then Jesus prayed to the Father and asked Him to send the Holy Spirit to us. The Holy Spirit is our gift from the Father and represents Jesus every moment of our lives. The Holy Spirit wants to be with us and in us, never leaving us alone. He longs for us to know Him more intimately and learn how to surrender fully to His control, direction, and protection.

Like all things on this earth, we must learn to develop into the person we were created to be with the Holy Spirit within us. The Holy Spirit is our gift. May we never misuse, ignore, or blaspheme our precious Holy Spirit. Use this time as you journey through the pages learning and experiencing more of the Holy Spirit and Who He is. Learn how to release all nine gifts and all nine manifestations of His fruit within you.

Don't hurry and get in a rush. Take your time. Learn to pray, be still, listen, and learn from the Holy Spirit who has been given to help you! This is not a race, and on this earth we are not even running to a finish line. We are not competing with another human! We are learning to walk with the Holy Spirit. When you need to run, He will tell you. There is no need to hurry; there is only the need to learn to be with the Holy Spirit. He is the teacher and the counselor. He is your guide and your constant companion.

Be honest with yourself and with the Lord when you are answering the questions. Many of the questions are not as much information as they are impartation experiences. This workbook is for you! No one is going to grade your answers or say this answer is wrong or right. You are with Your Father, and He will show you every step of the way. Don't be afraid. Just begin the journey. He will walk every page with you and then right into eternity!

Introduction

Who is the Holy Spirit to you?

_____
_____
_____
_____
_____
_____
_____

Would you like to know the Holy Spirit more intimately?

_____
_____
_____
_____
_____
_____
_____
_____

Which one of the Godhead is the Holy Spirit?

_____
_____
_____
_____

Where is the first mentioned scripture of the Holy Spirit?

_____
_____
_____
_____
_____

Jesus taught that the Holy Spirit would be His what?

List some of the names of the Holy Spirit both in the Old Testament and the New Testament.

Chapter One
Who Is the Holy Spirit?

Can you think of instances throughout your life when the Holy Spirit was with you and you didn't realize it until later? Write out a few of those times to remind yourself that He never leaves you or forsakes you.

_____
_____
_____
_____
_____
_____
_____
_____
_____
_____

How does He speak to you? Do you hear His voice either audibly or in your spirit? Do you feel His presence guide you? Do you feel an impression? Explain how the Holy Spirit has led you?

_____
_____
_____
_____
_____
_____
_____
_____
_____
_____

Matthew 5:6 tells us in what position we can put ourselves to bring the Holy Spirit and His righteousness in our lives. What can you do? What is your part in receiving "satisfaction" from heaven?

_____
_____
_____
_____
_____
_____
_____
_____

Isaiah 55:1-2 tells even more details of what you can do to bring a greater dimension of the Holy Spirit into your life. Explain what you can do to bring about a position that causes your soul to delight itself in fatness or spiritual joy.

___

As expressed in Leviticus 9:23, what is "the glory"?

___

Would that same "glory" be available for us today? How so?

___

How can we change our individual nation? What can you do as your part in changing the nation for God?

What is the definition in your own words of the Hebrew word "doxa"?

In relationship to what has transpired over the last few years with the worldwide Covid-19 pandemic, what is the name of the Holy Spirit that can change a person's breath?

In your own words define "Ruach."

Who is the Holy Spirit to you daily?

Do you want to experience Him more deeply? Explain.

Chapter Two
Where Does the Holy Spirit Live?

Where is the Holy Spirit within you?

How long have you made Him wait for you?

In Matthew 6:6 NKJV, how many times does it list "you" and "your"?

Would you say that you hold the key to the secret place within you?

What position has the Holy Spirit as the Father's representative played in your secret place?

Jesus gave us a promise of the Holy Spirit in John 14. Who did Jesus say that the Holy Spirit would be for us? The Holy Spirit will be your:

One of the last things Jesus said before He ascended was a reiteration of the coming of the Holy Spirit (Acts 1:8). What did Jesus promise we would all receive when we receive the Holy Spirit?

_____
_____
_____

Once you receive this gift of the Holy Spirit and His power, then you step into position to become a _____ for Jesus Christ! Have you fulfilled this in your daily life? Please explain and give examples of how you have done this.

_____
_____
_____
_____
_____
_____
_____
_____
_____
_____

What was your first encounter with the Holy Spirit? If it is in this book, please write out what you are already experiencing with the Holy Spirit.

_____
_____
_____
_____
_____
_____

What did I do to prepare myself to receive my healing?

_____
_____
_____
_____
_____
_____

When they received the Holy Spirit in Acts 2:1-4, were they quiet about it?

How did the Holy Spirit express Himself through the 120 people who had assembled in unity while they waited for this gift that Jesus promised from Father God?

According to the verses in Acts 2, did they all receive the Holy Spirit? Did they all speak in tongues?

When they received the Holy Spirit, where did He go?

Where does the Holy Spirit live now within humanity?

Does He live inside every human?

What is the condition that causes the Holy Spirit to move inside a person?

What must we do to have the Holy Spirit live within us?
_____
_____
_____

What must you do to have the Holy Spirit live within you?
_____
_____
_____

Chapter Three
How Do I Receive the Holy Spirit?

If you have received the Holy Spirit, go ahead and journal that experience as you remember it. Allow the Holy Spirit to help you remember from His perspective.

_____
_____
_____
_____
_____
_____
_____

If you have not yet received the Holy Spirit, just hold on; we will get to that!

As a little Methodist girl, what did I confess regularly that allowed my spirit to be open to receive the Holy Spirit when I was 17 years old?

_____
_____
_____
_____

According to John 14 through the teachings of Jesus to His disciples, how do you receive the Holy Spirit?

_____
_____
_____
_____

What is your part in allowing the Holy Spirit to come and live inside your spirit?

_____
_____
_____
_____

What must you conquer to walk fully Spirit-led all the days of your life?

_____
_____
_____
_____

You are made of three parts. Name those three parts and then explain where the Holy Spirit resides within you.

_____
_____
_____
_____
_____

To allow the Holy Spirit to move inside my spirit, I must bring both my flesh and soul (mind, will, and emotions) under subjection to my spirit. To keep my spirit in the lead, what can I do to help strengthen who I really am (spirit) and conquer my carnal body and mind?

_____
_____
_____
_____
_____

_____ and _____ can keep you in a prison all their own. How do you keep from doing these two things?

_____
_____
_____
_____

Let me ask you again, how do you receive the Holy Spirit?

_____
_____
_____
_____

Have you given your life to Jesus? Is He your Savior and your Lord? Write it out in detail. Give me the who, what, when, where, how version of your salvation experience?

_____
_____
_____

Have you been water baptized? _____

Water baptism doesn't make you any more or any less saved, but why would you not want to do the same thing if Jesus did it?

_____
_____

Would you like to be baptized in water if you haven't been? _____
Then make it happen!

When you are truly converted from your old person to your new eternal being, what happened to your old person?

_____
_____
_____

Is Jesus Christ truly the Lord of every area of your life?

_____
_____
_____
_____

Romans 10:9 tells us to _____ and _____ with our mouths that Jesus Christ is Lord, and in our _____ we must believe that God raised Jesus from the dead to be _____. Do you believe this? Have you confessed this? How often do you share and witness this to others?

_____
_____
_____
_____
_____

Jesus Christ will not make you do anything. You must choose Him as _____ and _____.

The first step in receiving the Holy Spirit is to be saved, truly saved. If you have not made that decision, let's stop right now and pray this prayer. If you have made the decision and Jesus is your Lord and Savior, then you may want to stop and rededicate your life to Him again. It's like renewing your vows. He is your Bridegroom and you are His bride (whether you are male or female, you still belong to Him)! Take a moment to talk to Jesus and state or restate your commitment to Him. If you have never prayed the prayer to give your life to Jesus, then pray this prayer right now.

Prayer of Salvation

If you have never made Jesus the Lord of your life, or if you would like to re-dedicate your life to Him, please pray this prayer of salvation.

Heavenly Father, I come to You admitting that I am a sinner. Right now, I choose to turn away from sin and I ask You to cleanse me of all unrighteousness. I believe that Your Son, Jesus, died on the cross to take away my sins. I also believe that He rose again from the dead so that I might be forgiven of my sins and be made righteous through faith in Him. I call upon the name of Jesus Christ to be the Lord and Savior of my life. Jesus, I choose to follow You and I ask that You fill me with the power of the Holy Spirit. I declare right now that I am a child of God! I am free from sin and full of the righteousness of God. I am saved, in Jesus' name. Amen.

Isn't it wonderful to get everything in place in your life? I suspect that no matter who you were before you were saved, you were not nearly as "ungodly" as Saul who became Paul. Paul had an amazing conversion experience. When Paul was filled with the Holy Spirit, he went everywhere looking for people to pray for the baptism of the Holy Spirit. In Acts 19 Paul was traveling as an evangelist and looking for believers. When he found 12 men who professed they were believers, what were his first words?

_____
_____
_____

Are you as excited as Paul to share the baptism of the Holy Spirit with everyone you meet? He could not wait to pray with people to receive the Holy Spirit. Explain why you are or you are not excited to pray with people to receive the baptism of the Holy Spirit.

_____
_____
_____
_____

Whatever you are looking for, you will find. What are you looking for at this point in your life?

_____
_____
_____
_____

Paul baptized them in the name of the Lord Jesus and then did something else? What did he do?

___

Did they all receive the Holy Spirit? What was the evidence that they had truly been baptized in the Holy Spirit?

___

That is also your evidence. Just as it was the evidence for the 120 that were in the upper room and for the 12 men that Paul prayed for, so it is with you. When you are baptized in the Holy Spirit, you will have evidence that will stand in the court of heaven and earth for all eternity. What is that evidence?

___

State in your own words the difference between gathering and assembling.

___

By humanity receiving the Holy Spirit, we can truly assemble as one body of believers because of the very Godhead Holy Spirit living within us. When we receive the Holy Spirit, the very breath of God moves within our being. How does that make you feel to understand that the power of the living God now lives within you?

___

Who gives the Holy Spirit?
_____

How is the Holy Spirit represented on earth to humanity?
_____
_____

According to Luke 11:13, what do we need to do to receive the Holy Spirit?
_____
_____

What are some simple steps you must do to receive the Holy Spirit?
_____
_____

When the Holy Spirit moves from "with me" to "in me," what is the one part of my human body that is totally changed? (Hint! James 3)
I go from having an untamable _____ to having a fire _____!

Once I finally yield myself fully to the Holy Spirit's control, He can now play me like an _____. I must continue to choose every day of my life whether to yield to _____ or yield to _____. (Romans 6:13)

Whatever or whoever you yield to will always play you. Your sound will come from who you allow to play you, including your own flesh.

Would you like to ask the Holy Spirit to reside within you for the rest of your days? Are you ready to house the very living God inside your spirit? Once you do, your speaking, singing, worshiping and literally everything that comes out of your mouth should change for the better! You will sound like the language of heaven and no longer sound like earth.
_____
_____
_____

Let's keep going and see how deep you are willing to go!

Chapter Four
What Is the Work of the Holy Spirit?

The Holy Spirit has many assignments to accomplish on earth. He can only move through humanity where He is housed. According to Galatians 3:5, the Holy Spirit works _____ and _____. It is not through the Law that these two works are released but through our _____.

According to Romans 8:26, the Holy Spirit comes to _____ and _____ in our weakness. This particular verse gives us clarity of how the Holy Spirit prays through us when we are too weak to pray the will of the Lord to the earth. We really don't know what to pray or how to pray heaven to earth without the voice of the Holy Spirit praying through us. What are you holding on to—situations, circumstances, people, family—that you have been afraid to allow the Holy Spirit to pray the will of the Lord? You will know them when you start to name them, and they may even be people or circumstances you have held in your own "control" rather than trusting the Holy Spirit to bring forth God's will. Write them out and repent of not trusting the Holy Spirit; then release whatever you are holding on to and let it go. Now pray in the Holy Spirit and let God do the work necessary to accomplish His will through your prayers.

_____
_____
_____
_____
_____
_____
_____
_____
_____
_____
_____
_____
_____
_____
_____
_____
_____
_____
_____
_____
_____
_____

The main work of the Holy Spirit through us is _____. When we are too weak, scared, fearful, etc. to do this, He will do it through us! God's Word promises that the Holy Spirit will bear us up and come to our aid! We must allow Him to do so.

In the court of heaven, Jesus calls the Holy Spirit our _____. He works alongside Jesus as our defense attorney and helps us.

Whenever we feel like we can't hear the Holy Spirit, we can _____ and _____ to help us be able to hear His voice more clearly. (Acts 13:2)

Who searches your heart?
_____
_____
_____

Who intercedes and pleads before God on your behalf?
_____
_____
_____

The Holy Spirit is given to us from _____. How He must love us to give us one of the triune Godhead to live within us here to help in our weaknesses.

The work of the Holy Spirit through us is listed as nine different attributes called fruit. What are those nine manifested harvests (fruits)?

1. _____
2. _____
3. _____
4. _____
5. _____
6. _____
7. _____
8. _____
9. _____

Harvests seem like a wonderful word unless you grew up on a farm like me. Then you will know that whether you are planting, cultivating, preparing, weeding, or harvesting it all takes a lot of work. But the great part about harvest is that it's the finish line for that particular race (seed-time-harvest). Plus, once the harvest is in, the "fruit of your labor" has great rewards. Walking in the fruit of the Holy Spirit is no different. It isn't fairy dust or somebody praying enough to have the fruit of the Holy Spirit. It takes a lot of work on our part to get to the place where we are "fruiting" the harvest.

Jesus taught His disciples about the work of the Holy Spirit that would be given soon after His resurrection. He gave them detailed descriptions of the personal work of the Holy Spirit. He shared with them exactly who the Holy Spirit would be to them personally! In your own words list those attributes (works) of the Holy Spirit and how each one has touched you personally in your own walk with the Lord through His Spirit. (John 14)

_____
_____
_____
_____
_____
_____
_____
_____
_____
_____
_____
_____
_____

The Holy Spirit is the representative of _____.

The Holy Spirit has been sent to take _____ place.

The Holy Spirit is my _____
_____
_____
_____
_____
_____
_____
_____
_____
_____
_____
_____
_____
_____
_____

The Holy Spirit _____, _____, _____, and is always on _____ ready to help me.
I can always count on the Holy Spirit to tell me the _____ because He is the Spirit of _____.

I can't see or receive the Holy Spirit if I am worldly. When I am born again, I am a new creature IN CHRIST; old things (world things) are passed away. If you say you love Jesus but you are still worldly, what does that tell you about your so-called salvation experience?

Is it possible to have an encounter with Jesus without being truly converted?

Is it possible to be convicted and still not change?

Do you want all the work of the Holy Spirit in your life? If you just said yes, then what must you do today, right now, to walk with Him fully?

What must you lay down at His feet to be completely "His" from this moment forward?

Most people want a ticket to heaven but don't want to be thrown into the fire of His presence. Has that been you before today? If so, stop and repent and ask the Lord to renew a right spirit within you.

_____
_____

What can you do to hear His voice more clearly?

_____
_____
_____
_____

God's Word is alive and full of power. His Word is sharper than any two-edged sword. What must His Word divide within you so that you can more fully move and house His presence?

_____
_____
_____
_____

What have you said "yes" to in your life that in hindsight you realize should have been "no"?

_____
_____
_____

What have you said "no" to that in hindsight you realize should have been "yes"?

_____
_____
_____

Recall times in your walk with the Holy Spirit that you knew what He wanted you to do and was leading you to do, but you chose to disobey?

_____
_____
_____
_____

Isn't hindsight amazing? Father, help us "come up higher" with You and take our seat beside You so we can see clearly our future as we walk more in tune with the Holy Spirit.

Can you think of moments in your life when you have heard statements similar to "before they become like you, you will become like them"? Explain please.

_____
_____
_____
_____
_____
_____
_____
_____
_____
_____
_____

Chapter Five
How Do I Yield to the Holy Spirit?

Yielding to the Holy Spirit is a matter of my own _____. I must choose fully and completely before the triune God Holy Spirit will move in and live within me.

Holy Spirit wants to play me like His _____. I must yield to the Holy Spirit to be His _____.

According to Romans 6:12-13, I can either yield myself to _____ or to _____. It is my choice whether I am played by the demonic forces or by the Holy Spirit.

How do you yield to the Holy Spirit?

_____
_____
_____
_____

What is the one thing you can do for the rest of your life that creates a constant flow of the Holy Spirit? (Hint! It's the same thing that makes you a great musician!)

_____
_____
_____
_____
_____

You are in control of the secret place of your life. We have discussed this already from Matthew 6:6. But You, when You pray, go into Your most private room. Shut your door. You are in control of your experience in your own secret place. Once you understand this, you will no longer beg the Holy Spirit to be with you because you will realize He already lives inside you. You are the one who either chooses or doesn't choose to meet Him in the secret place that you control. What can you do differently from this day forward to make sure you are yielded more and more each day? This is personal. This is about you. No one knows you better than you do, so be honest with yourself. Knowing that the Holy Spirit sees every word you write, explain below how you can better belong to Him and yield to Him each day.

_____
_____
_____
_____

When Jesus received the Holy Spirit as a dove descending from heaven, John heard a voice from heaven. What did the Father have to say that John audibly heard?

___

Can you imagine what it must have been like for John the Baptizer to hear the sound of the Father's voice audibly? How would you feel if you heard the audible voice of your Father God?

___

Once you fully yield to the Holy Spirit, what is your position where your own will is concerned? Explain what that means to you.

___

Should we yield to a "voice" we don't personally know? How can we know Him more to yield more of ourselves to Him?

___

When the announcement comes—"Behold, the Bridegroom"—Go out to meet Him!"- will you be ready to meet Him?

___

What did the foolish virgins want from the wise virgins?

___

Do you have people in your life that prefer you do their "spiritual" work for them?
_____
_____
_____

Have you leaned on others to do the spiritual work for you?
_____
_____
_____

What have you learned from this story in Matthew 25 that you can apply to your own personal relationship with Jesus Christ and His Holy Spirit?
_____
_____
_____
_____

What do the lamps represent in their lives?
_____
_____
_____

What does the oil represent?
_____
_____
_____

In verses 9-13 the wise told those who didn't have enough oil to "go to the dealers and buy for yourselves" more oil. So, there is a substitute for the real deal of the Holy Spirit. A counterfeit, so to speak, can be bought that looks like, feels like, and even acts like the oil of the Holy Spirit. But apparently it isn't good enough to make the Bridegroom wait on you, because once they returned with their substitute oil, the door was already shut and the Bridegroom had gone with those that had the legitimate Holy Spirit oil. The Bridegroom in this story had only gone as far as the other side of the door. Those with the substitute oil had a conversation with the Bridegroom through the already closed door. Not only had they just missed him, but they also had purchased something at a high price when they could have had it in abundance if they had been wise at the right time.

How heartbreaking to be so very close to the One who died for you, laid His life down for you, sent you His replacement through the Holy Spirit, and lives for you now only to hear that your costly substitute still won't make Him wait or open the door after you missed the timeline. You may still be praying and conversing, but it doesn't mean you are together.

How does this make you feel? Would you like to write something right now to your Bridegroom?

_____
_____
_____
_____
_____
_____
_____
_____
_____

Would you like to stop and ask the Holy Spirit for more oil of His presence? Write what your heart is saying right now.

_____
_____
_____
_____
_____

Can you put off until tomorrow what the Holy Spirit is telling you to do today? What is delayed obedience?

_____
_____

Jesus should have come already as far as I am concerned. Our daughter went to heaven in November of 1999 and every day since then has been too long for me to wait. I am looking for His return. I am praying for His return. I want to be with Him. It's been over two decades now, and I remain vigilant as I wait for His return. I have more oil now than I did in 1999. When reading the story in 2 Kings 4, how does that apply to your own life and keeping your oil increasing and flowing?

_____
_____
_____
_____

What can you do to remain in a constant steady increase of Holy Spirit oil flowing in your personal life and ministry?
_____
_____
_____
_____
_____
_____

Did the prophet tell her to borrow oil?
_____
_____
_____

What did he tell her to borrow?
_____
_____
_____

Explain in your own personal life what this could mean for you?
_____
_____
_____

Don't forget to yield to the Holy Spirit. It is vital for your continued growth.

Chapter Six
What Are the Gifts of the Holy Spirit?

The Holy Spirit has a manifestation number and a designated number. I like to call his manifestation number His heavenly number because it began with His covering over Lucifer and still holds through His covering and indwelling of us. What is that manifested number?

_____

The Holy Spirit's designated number was when He was given to the earth after Jesus's resurrection. What is that number? _____

What does the Bible call these nine manifestations of the gifts of the Holy Spirit?

_____
_____
_____
_____

The writer of Corinthians, Paul, wrote that he did not want you to be misinformed about the gifts of the Holy Spirit. Do you believe you are well informed on the gifts of the Holy Spirit? Please explain your answer.

_____
_____
_____
_____
_____
_____
_____
_____
_____
_____
_____

Why do some people fear the manifestations of the gifts of the Holy Spirit?

_____
_____
_____
_____
_____
_____
_____

When you are truly being used by the Holy Spirit, what can you not say?

_____
_____
_____

Out of the abundance of the heart the _____.

The gifts of the Holy Spirit come with the package of the Holy Spirit, so why would a person say they want the Holy Spirit but then reject all His gifts?

_____
_____
_____

What is one of the easiest ways to know what is in another person's heart?

_____
_____
_____

How can we know if a person is truly under the influence of the Holy Spirit?

_____
_____
_____

When we are fully yielded to the Holy Spirit, our lives will produce _____ just like in a courtroom. What kind of evidence is proving who controls you? Just write about you for a moment. What manifestations come forth out of your life that is enough evidence to prove the Holy Spirit's control over you?

_____
_____
_____
_____
_____
_____
_____
_____
_____

Why do you suppose the tongue of fire was given and shown to all in the first worldwide giving of the Holy Spirit in Acts 2?

_____
_____
_____
_____

Do you feel that same "tongue of fire" is evidenced when a person gets filled with the Holy Spirit today? Why or why not?

_____
_____
_____
_____
_____
_____
_____
_____

What are some of the expressions of who you are? For example, I am a girl, a wife, a mother, a minister, etc.). Who are you?

_____
_____
_____
_____
_____
_____
_____
_____

List the nine gifts of the Holy Spirit.
1. _____
2. _____
3. _____
4. _____
5. _____
6. _____
7. _____
8. _____
9. _____

Once you have received the Holy Spirit, how can you be sure you have all nine gifts within you?

_____
_____
_____
_____
_____
_____
_____

Who is the instrument? _____

Who is the Musician? _____

What can the Holy Spirit do to fear? _____

Will the Holy Spirit manifest without a human today?
_____
_____

Peter was completely changed once he was filled with the Holy Spirit and received his "new fire tongue." He came out of the upper room and began to do what to thousands of people?
_____
_____
_____
_____

How many were converted to Christ that day?
_____
_____

For those in our culture that try and promote that altar calls or "counting hands" is antiquated and out of date for today's church, what would they have said to Peter that day? Culture may change and the way a message is delivered may change. The dress code for the pulpit may continually shift, but the altar should never change! People need an opportunity to repent and give their lives to Jesus Christ. Peter obviously didn't get the memo that he was not supposed to give an altar call or embarrass the audience since we know from the Bible that 3,000 people gave their lives to Christ in that one day. Somebody counted!

Paul was so on fire once he was filled with the Holy Spirit that he went looking for other believers to share his experience with them! Paul, who had persecuted many Christians, and even held the coats of those who stoned Stephen, was completely changed in his nature once he was baptized in the Holy Spirit. When he found his fellow Christians in Acts 19 what was his first question to them?

_____
_____

When you receive the Holy Spirit, you also receive _____! That infilling power of the Holy Spirit causes you to be a great _____ for Jesus to all the world.

The gifts of the Holy Spirit don't come and go. They don't wane or lose their power. People do. People lose their fire, their power, their witness. People think that culture controls the church, and it may control *your* church, but culture doesn't control *the* church. The Holy Spirit controls His church. If you are not controlled by the Holy Spirit, then maybe you are not in *His* church!

The Holy Spirit is not mental, emotional, religious, or physical. The Holy Spirit is spirit. He doesn't need my help. He needs my _____.

As wonderful as the gifts of the Holy Spirit are, we are not to seek them. We are only to seek _____.

Your body is the temple of the Holy Spirit once you ask Him to come and live inside you. What do you need to do differently to take good care of His temple? This could be mentally, physically, emotionally, and spiritually? Ask Him to show you what you can do to improve His temple.

_____
_____
_____

The Holy Spirit does not need us to represent Him. He needs us to _____.

Did you pray the prayer in the book? Is there anything you would like to add now in your prayer?

_____
_____
_____
_____
_____

Chapter Seven
What Is the Fruit of the Holy Spirit?

What is opposed to the Holy Spirit?

What creates your ability not to be subject to the Law?

What are the practices of the flesh? The Bible lists them, and you may have a few of your own to add to the list.

Those who do such things—these actions of the flesh—shall not inherit the kingdom of God. Do you think that means that a person who is still operating in the flesh won't go to heaven? Why or why not?

The fruit of the Holy Spirit is the opposite of the works of the flesh. The fruit of the Holy Spirit helps our earthly lives be more enjoyable for us and for others. How does walking in the fruit of the Holy Spirit help you daily? Explain please, using each nine segments of the Holy Spirit's fruit.

We tend to categorize the works of the flesh as some not so bad but others really horrible! What works of the flesh listed in Galatians 5 have you been dismissing as just a part of normal life or perhaps just the way it is today in our culture?

_____
_____
_____

After reading what the Bible says about the works of the flesh, do you feel anything in the list is permissible to dismiss? _____

If you answered no, and I assume you did, then how will you deal with things like selfishness in a society that constantly promotes "self-love," "self-care," and a "gotta take care of me" mentality?

_____
_____
_____
_____

What about jealousy, strife, and anger? These seem to be totally permissible in our society today. We allow the world's systems to divide God's people over literally anything and everything! We must guard our hearts and our minds not to fall into the trap of the devil's game to divide and conquer. How can you protect yourself from these types of situations after studying the verses in Galatians?

_____
_____
_____
_____
_____

Fruit is singular in the phrase "fruit of the Holy Spirit." Therefore, we must assume that when we receive the Holy Spirit not only do we receive all nine of His manifested gifts when He wants any one of them to manifest, but we also receive the ability to house all nine segments of the fruit of the Holy Spirit. We have the ability to have love, joy, peace, patience, kindness, goodness, faithfulness, gentleness, and self-control from within our spirits. This is not from our own natural abilities to love or be joyful or filled with peace. This is beyond our natural ability. When nothing is left of our patience and we fruit patience, that's when you can be certain you are in harvest time of the Holy Spirit and His fruit is bursting forth! Can you think of times in your life when you were most definitely fruiting the Holy Spirit and not your own personality? Explain.

After reading through the list of works of the flesh, I am convicted each time to stop and repent! It seems that no matter how long I walk with the Lord or how long I have the Holy Spirit residing in my temple (body), I find myself operating from the works of the flesh more often than I ever care to admit. When I wrote this book, I had to stop and repent. Each time I edited it (which is several times before we ever go to print), I had to stop and repent. While writing this companion workbook, I had to stop and repent again! We are housed in flesh, but we must not be walking in the manifestation of our flesh! How do we stop "fruiting flesh"? I don't know. If you figure it out, please let me know! I do know for certain that as long as I am in a flesh body, I am so very thankful for the ability to be able to repent before my Father God in the name of Jesus. I am forever thankful for my Advocate who stands in the gap for me before the Righteous Judge. Would you like to stop for a moment and bow your knee before the King also? Repent if you need to and come from His feet clean and holy once again without the smell of "flesh" on you.

In 2 Timothy 3 we see a prophetic chapter on the time in which we are living now! What is the main issue that you see when reading this prophetic chapter? Do you see a thread in the chapter that coincides with the thread of the degradation of our own society today? Explain.

What is opposed to the Holy Spirit?

_____
_____
_____
_____

List the nine segments of the fruit of the Holy Spirit in the order that the Bible gives them.
1. _____
2. _____
3. _____
4. _____
5. _____
6. _____
7. _____
8. _____
9. _____

Without the Holy Spirit living within us, we are hopeless to produce anything other than our _____. With the Holy Spirit living within us, we can produce His _____ instead of our own _____.

The Bible says that love covers a multitude of sins. What is a good way to check the fruit of love in your own life?

_____
_____
_____
_____
_____
_____

When you are walking in love, your first response is to _____, not to expose others.

If you are not fruiting joy, how do you feel without joy? What is missing in your life at that point?

_____
_____
_____
_____

What if each fruiting season builds upon the next? What if you can't truly find joy until you learn to operate in the love of the Lord? What if peace will never come in your life until you learn how to love others and exude the joy of the Lord? Can you see the levels of fruit as building floors of the "temple of the Holy Spirit" in your own life? If that is the case, and I believe it is, then you can never truly get to the top floor of your temple of self-control until you learn how to build the first eight floors. What does this mean to you in your everyday life?

_____
_____
_____
_____
_____

What do you feel you need to work on more within yourself?

_____
_____
_____
_____
_____

It is no wonder that even in the society of what we call "church world" there is very little self-control, and that is the final "floor" of the temple of the Holy Spirit within us. In which levels (floors) do you need more submission to the Holy Spirit to build a strong foundation for His temple? Please explain.

_____
_____
_____
_____
_____

According to the Bible, mastering the foundational floor (fruit) of love seems to be the greatest priority. The Bible says we should _____ one another and we can know that we have passed over out of death into Life by the fact that we _____ the brethren.

1 John 3 clearly states that the way to know and understand and have the proof that He really lives and makes His home in us is not by speaking in tongues, even though you will speak in tongues when the Holy Spirit moves within you. The greatest evidence of His presence within us is when we keep His commandments and we _____.

When you are truly housing the Holy Spirit within you, love is your first response to others.

Every scripture is _____ and profitable for _____, for reproof and _____ of sin. We need God's Word to help us live and walk in love. The Holy Spirit within us helps us by convicting us, correcting us, helping us, and training us in righteousness. Can you see how this has been a part of your life walking with the Holy Spirit? Please explain.

_____
_____
_____
_____
_____

Chapter Eight
The Correlation Between the Fruit and the Gifts of the Holy Spirit

List the nine fruit of the Holy Spirit and beside each one, in the order given in the Bible, list the gifts of the Holy Spirit.

1. _____   1. _____
2. _____   2. _____
3. _____   3. _____
4. _____   4. _____
5. _____   5. _____
6. _____   6. _____
7. _____   7. _____
8. _____   8. _____
9. _____   9. _____

Have you considered that once you develop the fruit of the Holy Spirit, His gifts could manifest more readily from within you?

_____
_____
_____
_____

With that thought in mind as you develop your love foundation, your mouth would more readily speak the Word of Wisdom rather than whatever might roll out of your mind or emotions. A strong love walk would create a mind controlled by the Holy Spirit and automatically make you wiser because you are no longer being controlled by your own flesh or soul. Your spirit, controlled by the Holy Spirit, is light years ahead of your flesh and soul realms. With that revelation within you, why would you ever resist the flow of the Holy Spirit? You are smarter, wiser, more powerful and more wonderful when the Holy Spirit is leading your life (and your mouth)! Then why do you sometimes resist Him?

_____
_____
_____
_____
_____
_____
_____
_____

The gifts of the Holy Spirit when manifesting benefit _____.

The fruit of the Holy Spirit when manifesting benefit _____.

Is it possible for someone to flow in the gifts of the Holy Spirit and not show any signs of the fruit of the Holy Spirit in their lives? Please explain.

___

Do you personally feel that the Father would be impressed by this or disappointed by this? Please explain.

___

The Bible says in Matthew 7:16, *You will fully recognize them by their fruits.* Then scripture says again in Matthew 7:20, *"Therefore, you will fully know them by their fruits."* When a person is fruiting the Holy Spirit, the scripture plainly tells us that we can "know" them by their fruit. It doesn't say that we can know them by their gifts. What does this mean to you?

___

The fruit of the Holy Spirit and the gifts of the Holy Spirit are both precious gifts from the Father to us. People tend to run after the _____. People don't tend to want to spend time to develop the _____, which takes a great deal of time to be planted within us because it needs time to grow, mature, and ripen. Why do you think, as a general rule, people want to manifest the Holy Spirit's gifts but don't spend time to develop His fruit? Explain please. If possible, use your own life as an example.

What are you going to do about that?

What is the difference between my own personality traits and the fruit of the Holy Spirit?

1 Corinthians 13:13 states that three things—faith, hope, and love—abide in us when we walk in relationship with the Lord. It states that one is by far the most valuable. Which is it and explain why you believe it is the most valuable.

Revelation 21:19-20 lists foundation stones in the city wall of the bride of Christ. What are those 12 foundation stones?
    1. _____
    2. _____

3. _____
4. _____
5. _____
6. _____
7. _____
8. _____
9. _____
10. _____
11. _____
12. _____

What does the number 12 mean in ancient Hebrew? _____

Using the list of stones in Revelation 21 and the list of stones covering Lucifer in Ezekiel 28, can you name the nine common stones between these two lists?

1. _____
2. _____
3. _____
4. _____
5. _____
6. _____
7. _____
8. _____
9. _____

List from Exodus 28 the 12 stones (in order of four rows) in the High Priest's breastplate.
1st row 1. _____ 2. _____ 3. _____
2nd row 4. _____ 5. _____ 6. _____
3rd row 7. _____ 8. _____ 9. _____
4th row 10. _____ 11. _____ 12. _____

Notice that even though the name of some of the stones may vary from OT to NT, they are the same 12 stones but the order is different. What does that mean to you?

_____
_____
_____
_____
_____

It is the third row in the High Priest's breastplate that was missing in Lucifer's covering stones. God gave mankind a third row covering for His bride. Name the three stones in the third row of the High Priest's breastplate.

_____
_____
_____

The bride of Christ submits on all levels to become His full _____ and _____.

What stone is the first stone in the foundation stones of the bride and the last stone in the High Priest's breastplate?

_____
_____
_____

Who does this stone point us to?

_____
_____
_____

What scripture can we use to support this finding?

_____
_____

We can easily see Father God in the beginning of Genesis, and we can easily see the Holy Spirit in the first few verses. Where is Jesus, God's Son, in the beginning of the Bible?

_____
_____
_____

What is His name in the beginning, and you also can find that same name (title) in Revelation 19:13?

_____
_____
_____

I had you do this in the beginning of this chapter. Please do it again. List the nine fruit of the Holy Spirit and beside each one, in the order given in the Bible, list the gifts of the Holy Spirit.

1. _____ 1. _____
2. _____ 2. _____
3. _____ 3. _____
4. _____ 4. _____
5. _____ 5. _____
6. _____ 6. _____
7. _____ 7. _____
8. _____ 8. _____
9. _____ 9. _____

Can you see how each fruit could make each gift more powerful for the receiver of the manifested gift?
_____

Can you explain what is meant and use a few from the list as examples of what you mean?
_____
_____
_____
_____
_____
_____

When you spend time developing the fruit of the Holy Spirit in your life, you can help the gifts of the Holy Spirit to remain and flow for your lifetime. Do you agree with this? Explain either yes or no.
_____
_____
_____
_____
_____
_____

According to 1 Corinthians 12: 4-6, the gifts of the Holy Spirit flow within us due to the _____.

I have no reason to have any pride rise in me over any gifts of the Holy Spirit for it is not me at all. Why do you suppose anyone would fall trap to the same deception that Lucifer fell and lost his eternal archangel position? Explain your reasoning please.

_____
_____
_____
_____
_____
_____
_____
_____

Keep building your Holy Spirit foundations so that you will never fall into the same trap or deception as Satan. He will use the same things on you that caused him to fall if you are not careful. Be aware of the devil's plots and never give in to temptation. How can you keep yourself in your proper position to help maintain your God-given gifts of the Holy Spirit's fruit and gifts?

_____
_____
_____
_____
_____
_____
_____
_____

Chapter Nine
Jesus' Relationship With the Holy Spirit

When the Holy Spirit descended upon Jesus as He came up out of the water, was it in spirit or in the natural?

Who saw the dove?

Who heard the Father's voice?

Jesus was fully God and fully man. From the point of His baptism forward, He was fully controlled by the _____.

In the Book of Isaiah what did the Father prophesy that Jesus would bring forth to all nations?

Jesus showed us from the point of His baptism forward how we can walk in the Holy Spirit and be fully led by the Holy Spirit. Can you think of ways the Holy Spirit has led you in your walk with the Lord? Explain.

How many days did Jesus have to endure the devil's temptations?

What were some of the conditions that Jesus had to endure?

Who led Jesus into the wilderness to be tempted?

How did Jesus defeat the devil with each temptation?
_____

What one weapon that Jesus used to defeat the devil do you and I have today?
_____

Do you use this weapon every day as you should? Explain and give examples of how you use this weapon.
_____
_____
_____
_____
_____

After the devil realized he had lost this round with Jesus Christ, what did he do?
_____

What do you think the scripture means when it says that the devil waits for a more opportune and favorable time?
_____
_____
_____

Can you recall times in your life when the devil was waiting for you to get in a certain emotional or mental struggle to tempt you?
_____
_____
_____
_____
_____
_____
_____
_____

How old was Jesus by the time He was baptized? _____

Who baptized him? _____

What was the relationship between the two of them? _____

Did John want to baptize Jesus? _____

How did Jesus convince John to baptize Him?
_____

What is the formula for you to walk, talk, preach, teach, and heal like Jesus?
_____
_____
_____
_____
_____
_____

Are you willing to go through the trials, tests, and temptations Jesus went through to get to the point where the Father could use Him and the Holy Spirit could lead Him? Talk to your heavenly Father about this in the space below.
_____
_____
_____
_____
_____
_____
_____
_____

Does the Holy Spirit ever leave you? _____

Why are there times when "you feel" like He has left you? Explain.
_____
_____
_____
_____
_____
_____
_____

From where did the Holy Spirit come?

What came with the Holy Spirit?

How can you know you have experienced the infilling power of the Holy Spirit?

What natural manifestation happens for every person who receives the Holy Spirit?

When Jesus began to teach His disciples about the coming baptism of the Holy Spirit, He used many phrases to define, express, and explain what they could expect. List some of those adjectives here and explain how you have benefited with each of these Holy Spirit expressions.

How many ways are there to heaven?

What does the Bible say in John 14:5 about the way?

What was Jesus referring to when He said to the disciples that they already had the Holy Spirit with them but soon the Holy Spirit would be in them?

When I was crippled from a car wreck for six years, I used John 14:12-14 as proof from God's Word to build my spirit man in faith so I could receive my healing. Write these three verses here.

_____
_____
_____
_____
_____
_____

Now that you have written that passage of scripture, please explain what that passage means to you.

_____
_____
_____
_____

Because it is not enough to know who the Holy Spirit is, Jesus taught the disciples that one must "know" the Holy Spirit. Jesus taught about His personal divine relationship with the Holy Spirit and taught the disciples that they also could have that kind of relationship with the Holy Spirit. What is your part in walking fully led like Jesus with the Holy Spirit?

_____
_____
_____
_____

Jesus taught His disciples in John 14 that they could have relationships with all three of the Godhead: Father, Son, and Holy Spirit. Write here how you experience all three Godhead relationships in your own personal life.

Father _____
_____

Son _____
_____

Holy Spirit _____
_____

Why would we ever settle for less than a deep relationship when all three of the Godhead are available to us?

_____
_____

When the Holy Spirit was promised in Jesus' last words on earth in Acts 1:8, He promised that we shall receive_____
_____

If you say you are filled with the Holy Spirit but you do not have any power in your life, is it possible that you have had an experience (possibly emotional or mental) with the Holy Spirit but never really yielded to the full immersion of His baptizing presence?

_____
_____
_____
_____
_____

You may have many experiences without an immersion of the Holy Spirit. This is your choice and only you can fully decide what your future holds. Take time to pray and listen. Obey what you hear from the Holy Spirit.

One hundred and twenty people were fully baptized with the Holy Spirit in Acts 2 and had earthly evidence of this baptism through the voice and sound change coming from within them. They immediately began to _____
_____
_____
_____

Then in the next few verses we see that what they had received changed who they were to the point that we next see them in the scripture witnessing on the street! They are leading people to Jesus Christ as Lord and Savior. Are you doing this? _____

Jesus told His disciples that when they receive the Holy Spirit and His power fills them, they will have evidence (through tongues) and through their _____ of His infilling power.

Do you want to be like Jesus? Then you must _____.

In John 20:21-22 Jesus said that He was leaving something with them. What was it that He left with them? _____

Then Jesus breathed on them and said _____

Take a moment before you move into the next chapter to make sure you are fully surrendered to the Holy Spirit and filled to overflowing with His power. Here is a place to write your experience today.

_____
_____
_____
_____
_____
_____
_____
_____
_____
_____
_____
_____
_____

Chapter Ten
The Nature of the Spirit of God Is Fire

When the scripture says that God has proved us, tried us, and refined us, what does that mean to you?

_____
_____
_____
_____

Can you think of times in your life when you were certain you were being tried by fire? Explain.

_____
_____
_____
_____
_____
_____
_____
_____

When the Bible uses the phrase "the Spirit of God," to whom is that referring?

_____

God's nature is _____. He uses His nature to accomplish many things in our lives. List some of those outcomes when we submit to His fire.

_____
_____
_____
_____
_____
_____

List what happens when we don't submit to His fire.

_____
_____
_____
_____
_____

According to Psalm 97:3, we never want to be God's enemy because _____
_____
_____

According to Deuteronomy 4:24, our God is a _____.

When we are on God's side, He goes before us as a _____.

Have you noticed the position of God's fire in relation to His presence? Scripture always says that _____ goes before Him. God's fire burns up _____.

The Strong's Concordance gives us a very descriptive word in #H398. It is the word _____, which is the Hebrew word "akal." Write its meaning in your own words.
_____
_____
_____
_____
_____

The Hebrew word for fire is _____. It is the #H784 and its meaning is quite clear. Use your own words to define the word fire after reading the Strong's definition.
_____
_____
_____
_____
_____
_____

God coded His nature within the DNA of every human. He put within us His _____.

We are born with the ability to become His image. We can only be His image when we submit to His _____ and allow our image to reflect His image.

The fire nature of God was never meant to hurt us or harm us in any way! God's fire was meant to _____ us and make us _____.

When God has to use His fire as judgment, it is only because humanity has resisted becoming _____.

According to Matthew 25:41, He will have to say to those who are not at His right side _____.

The eternal fire was not prepared for humans. It was prepared for _____
_____.

The devil hates _____. He was created to worship God in the midst of the stones of fire, but instead of Lucifer submitting to God with his worship, pride turned him to look away from God to himself. Because he didn't stay in the position he was created by God to have forever, he will have to live forever in the _____ prepared for the _____ and his _____.

The devil hates fire. He hates God's fire in you. He hates the Holy Spirit's baptizing fire. Fire reminds him of his _____. Instead of accepting the purification of God's fire, he will have to accept the _____ of God's eternal lake of fire.

The devil made the statements of what I call the "five I wills." List those five condemning statements the devil made as listed in Isaiah 14.

_____
_____
_____
_____
_____
_____
_____
_____
_____
_____
_____
_____
_____

Before Lucifer's fall he had the ability to _____.

God set Lucifer in the midst of the _____ when He created him. Lucifer was covered with _____ and inside of him was _____.

Lucifer made choices that caused God to have to _____.
He lost his position over his choice to think he could be _____.

God made humanity with the ability to become the very image of God in the midst of His fire. Lucifer was created and positioned in the fire of God. He lost his eternal position by looking at himself instead of looking at His Creator. Make sure you keep your eyes on the Lord and don't be focusing on yourself! We can only be God's image when we don't resist His _____.

What was the speech given by one of the Hebrew teens in Daniel 3?
_____
_____
_____

Would you have the courage to say those words today?
_____
_____

We could be faced with just such a choice to make at any given moment. I am examining my heart and asking you to examine yours today. Talk to your Father God. Tell Him what you are thinking right now.
_____
_____
_____
_____
_____
_____

As you read the story in Daniel, did you feel as if the three teenagers were running out of the fire when the king called them to come out?
_____
_____
_____

Are you baptized in the Holy Spirit?
_____

Do you have the fire of the Holy Spirit in your life?
_____

Did the Lord rescue you time and time again from situations and circumstances you had gotten yourself into so you could long to be back in that place again?

_____

Even though you have not been turned into a pillar of salt, have you had moments in your life when you felt like you were drying up spiritually?

_____

With the Holy Spirit's help, take a look at those times and see if you can correlate your heart's longing for the worldly ways rather than the fire of God's presence. Explain.

_____
_____
_____
_____

Notice that the angels warned Lot and his family when they arrived at the little town of Zoar that they were to make haste and take refuge there. When you run to God's presence, don't stroll there! Don't visit His presence. Make haste! Run to His presence and when you get there, be still and know that He is God. Learn how to take refuge in His presence. Write your heart's feelings before the Father right now. Do you need to repent of looking more toward the world and its ways rather than to His presence?

_____
_____
_____
_____

The time is now. Please do not put off any longer this opportunity to run to Him and find your safe place in His presence. Stop for a moment and worship Him without an agenda of what you need.

_____
_____
_____
_____

We were created to go from _____ to _____. Looking back can bring about God's judgment fire. Don't look back! Be careful, _____, and _____.

What happens in the end to the beast and the false prophet?
_____
_____

What happens in the end to the devil, the beast, and the false prophet?
_____
_____

What happens in the end to death and hell?
_____
_____

You must make sure that _____ is written in His _____. Anyone whose name is not found in His Book of Life will be _____.

It's not good enough for you to know who Jesus is. He must know you. Write here how you know that He knows you!
_____
_____
_____
_____
_____
_____

Who will spend eternity in the lake of fire according to Revelation 21:8?
_____

What must you do if you find yourself on the list above?
_____

Elijah was a "fire prophet." He called fire down from heaven over and over again. In the story in 2 Kings 1, can you tell me what the third captain did to prevent himself and his men from being burned up in the fire?
_____
_____
_____

We can embrace God's fire nature and our lives will be _____ and _____ or we can spend eternity regretting what we did not do while here on earth.

When Moses encountered the fire nature of God, He was told not to come near and to _____.

God called the very ground where His fire nature burned _____ ground.

Where the Spirit of God is _____ remains.

We can either yield to God's purifying fire or we can be _____.

When God gave Moses the Ten Commandments, the mountain was on _____.

Wherever the Spirit of God is there will be _____. If you have the courage to house His Spirit within your flesh, you can be sure that all the remaining days of your life will be on _____.

Chapter Eleven
Three Baptisms: Water, Holy Spirit, and Fire

John the Baptist prophesied in Matthew 3 that Jesus was coming after him. John said that he baptized in water but Jesus would baptize with two more levels of baptism: the Holy Spirit and fire.

John had followers before Jesus had followers. John was Jesus' cousin. John's mother, Elizabeth, and Jesus' mother, Mary, were cousins. John and Jesus were family. There was a divine connection beyond their family ties. John was the forerunner of Jesus! He announced the coming of the Messiah! What a joy to know for all of eternity that you would be known as Jesus' announcer!

How would you feel if you were Jesus' cousin?
_____
_____
_____
_____

Do you think you could have fulfilled your destiny by announcing His coming as Messiah?
_____
_____

John prophesied the coming of Messiah and he also prophesied the coming of the Holy Spirit and heaven's fire! What a true prophet John was! He saw into the future, then further into the future, then further into the future!

John had a relationship with the Holy Spirit from his mother's_____, according to Luke 1. In fact, scripture says that John would be_____ the Holy Spirit even in and from his mother's womb. Can you imagine being filled with the Holy Spirit even in your mother's womb? _____

John was not concerned with _____ or concerned with _____. He never seemed concerned with his words hurting anyone's feelings or making them feel good about themselves.

Even though John knew that Jesus was the Messiah when Jesus came to him to be baptized, John _____.

When Jesus came up out of the water, three things happened that John witnessed.
1. _____
2. _____
3. _____

How would you feel or respond if you saw, heard, and witnessed this event?

_____
_____
_____
_____
_____
_____
_____
_____

Jesus' last words were recorded in Acts 1:8, and then angels followed His words with

_____
_____
_____
_____
_____
_____

When Jesus ascended and they journeyed into Jerusalem to "wait," how long did it take them to get there?

_____

After they arrived in Jerusalem and assembled in the upper room, how many days did they continue to wait?

_____

While they waited they replaced the fallen disciple, Judas, with _____.

They did not gather in the upper room. They assembled. Can you explain the difference?

_____
_____
_____
_____
_____

What can you count on to happen when you are truly baptized in the Holy Spirit? A _____ comes from heaven. A new _____ tongue sits on your head. You will begin to speak in tongues in a _____ and _____ expression of words.

After reading the statements above, have you ever noticed or considered that when a sound comes from heaven accompanied by a fire tongue that your own sound changes to the sound of heaven and your own tongue begins to feel like it is on fire? Explain your first experience of being baptized in the Holy Spirit?

_____
_____
_____
_____
_____
_____
_____

What changed for you?

_____
_____
_____
_____
_____

In what way can you describe your experience?

_____
_____
_____
_____
_____

Two separate baptisms happened in Acts 2. Explain each one please.

_____
_____
_____
_____
_____
_____

Can you explain how your experience with the Holy Spirit is also two separate baptisms?

_____
_____
_____

Isaiah was the _____ to the nation of Israel. It was his profession, his calling, and his responsibility. His uncle was the king and he died. As you read the story in Isaiah 6, can you share what you saw happen progressively to Isaiah in the very presence of the Lord?

Isaiah confessed that his lips were _____. He confessed that his eyes were beholding _____. Describe in your own detailed words Isaiah's "throne room experience."

Have you had similar experiences in God's presence?

What changed Isaiah's confession from "woe is me" to "send me?"

What did the angel use to touch Isaiah's tongue?

What has the Holy Spirit used to touch your life (even your tongue) and turn you around?

Notice I didn't say God caused something to happen to you; I said what has the Holy Spirit used. What the enemy has meant to harm us, God often uses to help us and create in us His fire of purification to get us on the right path. With that in mind, what has the Holy Spirit used the most in your life to continue to guide you, keep you, and protect you?

What is the "word picture" story that describes the word "repent"?
_____
_____
_____
_____
_____

How can you relate that original definition to your own life?
_____
_____
_____
_____

When we repent we are supposed to _____ and never ever look back at it again.

Repentance is not _____ or about saying _____.

Repentance is about change, true and real change. True repentance means that _____
_____
_____

Lot's wife never repented of longing for her past life. Looking back to your past can cost you your _____.

Why do the Jews celebrate Pentecost?
_____
_____
_____

Isn't it interesting that the giving of God's Ten Commandments (Word) and the giving of the Holy Spirit happened on the same Jewish celebration holiday. Can you see a correlation between the two events?

_____
_____
_____

Why is the third level of baptism, fire, so important in light of the depiction of our human flawed tongues in James 3?

_____
_____
_____
_____
_____
_____

What does James say our tongues do that ought not to be done?

_____
_____
_____

When we receive a new fire tongue from heaven, how does that help our untamable human tongue in which James spoke?

_____
_____
_____

A fire baptized tongue speaks with _____ and _____.

When we receive our third level of fire baptized tongue, we stop talking like the _____ and we stop sounding like the _____.

When you receive the third level of baptism of fire, your speech will _____.

If you are timid and shy, can being filled with the baptism of the Holy Spirit and fire change that for you?

_____
_____
_____

Can you remember moments, specific instances, or seasons when you knew that your tongue had changed from the "old way of talking" to a new tongue? Write it down to remind yourself of these times, events, and seasons.

_____
_____
_____

It's time to get a fresh baptism of fire. It may be time to renew all three levels of baptism in your life. If so, plan to be water baptized all over again, like a renewing of your vow to Jesus Christ. Ask the Father for a fresh infilling of the Holy Spirit and a new flood of His presence to fill you once again. Then, finally, ask the Father to baptize you in His fire and set you ablaze once again! It doesn't matter how long you have been saved or filled with the Holy Spirit if you are running cold instead of hot, powerless instead of powerful, and burned out instead of a fire walker, a fire talker, and a person on fire. It's time to ask the Father for a fresh personal revival of all three baptisms! Go ahead! Ask Him! He will give it to you. He promised He would! Write it out.

_____
_____
_____
_____
_____
_____
_____
_____
_____
_____
_____
_____
_____

Death and life are in the power of your _____. The devil is afraid of you when your tongue has been baptized with heaven's fire. When you talk with your fire tongue, you remind the devil of his _____.

The devil knows once you fully yield to the depths of water, Holy Spirit, and fire baptisms that you are prepared and created to take his original place as a fire walker in worship. Take your place, Holy Spirit worshiper!

Chapter Twelve
The Holy Spirit Speaks and Sings Through You

The Bible tells us plainly that the Holy Spirit wants to speak and sing! He wants to make His sound through you! Have you yielded your instrument, your vocal cords, and your breath to the Holy Spirit? _____

Have you allowed Him to speak through you? _____

Have you allowed Him to sing through you? _____

Have you yielded your instrument to be His in both tongues and interpretation? _____

What has been your biggest drawback in this area? _____

What questions arise that try to stop you from fully yielding in this area of singing and speaking in both tongues and interpretation?

_____
_____
_____
_____
_____
_____

In reading the article from Penn Medicine from 2006, what did you learn about the brain and the Holy Spirit within you?

_____
_____
_____
_____

What does your brain do or not do when you are speaking or singing in tongues?

_____
_____
_____

According to 1 Corinthians 14:4, who is edified and improved when you speak in tongues?

_____
_____
_____
_____

Can you explain why this is according to the article from the Penn Medical School study?

_____
_____
_____
_____
_____
_____
_____
_____
_____
_____

What is the one thing that you can do to help improve your self-worth and your self-image?

_____
_____
_____
_____
_____
_____
_____
_____
_____

Knowing that speaking and singing in tongues actually releases endorphins in the brain that produce an edifying sensation, why would we "try" to make ourselves feel better when we have the power of God within us to do this for us with no effort at all on our part? Jesus yielded to the Holy Spirit after He was baptized. He stayed in a prayerful position throughout the Biblical account of His ministry. Even to the very end in the Garden of Gethsemane when He fully yielded His will to the will of the Father, we can see the pattern to follow for our own lives. Why then would we think that once we yield ourselves we will stay yielded? Explain how you have had wrong thinking in this area; then explain how you can or have rectified this area of your thinking.

_____
_____
_____
_____
_____
_____
_____
_____
_____
_____
_____

You are the instrument. The Holy Spirit is the divine musician. He longs to play you to bring forth His sound to the earth and to humanity around you. Will you yield to Him today?

I want you to stop what you are doing and set the timer on your watch or phone for five minutes. Now pray in tongues for five minutes. Don't stop or look at your time. Pray without ceasing. Once the timer goes off, I want you to stop praying and write the interpretation here. You may say you don't have anything! You don't know what to write, etc. You receive the interpretation just like you receive the tongues. You don't have the tongues before you start speaking either. You just start speaking in tongues by using your faith. Now do the same with the interpretation. I hope you don't have an idea in your head because then it is probably "your idea." Just start writing like you just start speaking in tongues. Write until the flow stops. That is the interpretation. Go back and read it. It is probably a word from heaven for you personally.

Now set your timer for five minutes again. This time sing in tongues without ceasing for five minutes. After your timer goes off, stop singing in tongues and start writing the interpretation. Remember that you won't already have it in your head. The Holy Spirit does not filter what He wants to say through your thinking. The medical study showed that the brain doesn't even move or respond when speaking or singing in tongues. Once you start your interpretation, then your brain will begin to function because you are in a language your brain already knows. The key to keeping the interpretation pure and from God only is to keep your thinking to a minimum and your yielding to the Holy Spirit at a maximum! Now write the interpretation that you were singing for five minutes. It may come out as a song, lyrics, a poem, or just a flow from heaven to your pen and paper. Write beloved. Don't think, just write.

Chapter Thirteen
The Hierarchy of the Kingdom of God

This is one of the most recent deep revelations the Lord has shared with me. It came as a vision like a strike of lightning in my spirit's mind. I saw it all at once and have spent several years trying to slow it down enough to teach and share it with you.

After reading and studying this chapter and the layout of the ranking system of heaven, do you see where you fit? Do you see where your position is right now? Explain please.

_____
_____
_____
_____
_____
_____
_____
_____

What a powerful revelation to realize that once you yield to the Holy Spirit and are led by the Holy Spirit, you are now in the archangel position that Lucifer once held before his fall. The Holy Spirit was Lucifer's covering Godhead. The Holy Spirit is your covering Godhead. The Holy Spirit lives inside of you. You are His temple, His tabernacle! You are baptized in fire. Just as Lucifer walked among the stones of fire, you have that powerful heavenly fire within you. You are walking among the stones of fire, but even more importantly, you are the stones of fire! You house that fire! Everywhere you go, every sound you make, has the potential to bring "fire down from heaven" just like Elijah! Realizing who you are as His worshiper, write your thoughts. Tell the Father what you are feeling. Worship Him the way He deserves to be worshiped because you now own your position as His fire walking, talking, singing, shouting, worshiper! If a song comes forth, take the time to write it below. Whatever you feel in your heart and spirit, write it!

_____
_____
_____
_____
_____
_____
_____
_____
_____
_____
_____
_____
_____

When you worship, your Godhead covering is the Holy Spirit. When you are operating in the Word, declaring, decreeing, confessing, and believing, you are operating under the Father's covering. When you are warring in intercession, prayer, supplication, and worship, you are under Jesus Christ's covering. You are covered at all times by the triune Godhead!

Have you ever wondered how your relationship should work with all three positions of the Godhead? Now you can truly understand your position as you walk out your authority given to you by Jesus Christ. He left you in charge under the direction of Father God. Can you think of times when you have waited on the Lord only to realize that He was waiting on you? Explain.

_____
_____
_____
_____
_____
_____
_____

Why do you suppose when Jesus saw Lucifer fall, from heaven's viewpoint it looked like lightning?

_____
_____
_____
_____
_____
_____
_____

When Lucifer fell and became Satan, who did he take with him? How many did he take with him? (You may not find this in the book. You may have to look this up in the scripture.) Part of your training is to learn to think and research for yourself.

_____
_____
_____

What if all Bibles were confiscated today? Would there be enough Word of God in you to help you survive through the tribulation?

_____
_____

Memorize scripture. Don't just be a person who reads and forgets, but read and learn, memorize and meditate on scripture. Mull it over and over until the scripture is IN you!

Write below 10 of your favorite verses without looking them up. Don't forget the scriptural references that locate the verses.

Why is blaspheming the Holy Spirit unforgivable?

_____
_____
_____
_____

To see from God's perspective, we must think outside "the box," so to speak. We think and ultimately see horizontally. God sees and even speaks vertically. How can we learn to see from God's perspective?

_____
_____
_____
_____

Give at least one scripture to support your answer.

_____
_____
_____
_____

What ultimately happened to Lucifer to cause him to lose his eternal place in the midst of the throne room of Almighty God? Explain.

_____
_____
_____
_____

How can you prevent this happening to you?

_____
_____
_____
_____
_____

How many stones did Lucifer have as his covering in heaven? _____

Why did Lucifer have nine stones to cover him?

What is the correlation between Lucifer and the Holy Spirit, and how did you come to this conclusion? Please explain.

When Lucifer fell from heaven and was thrown to the earth, he lost many things. Can you list what he lost?

Did Jesus witness Lucifer's fall? What is the scripture reference and how did He describe it?

Is everyone saved who calls Jesus Lord?

What is the absolute certain way to know that you will enter the kingdom of heaven? (Hint: Matthew 7:21)

Is everything given from Father God good?

What was Father God's last and most significant "good gift" to humanity?

Jesus as our King and Prince also translates to Jesus as our _____. Who is the archangel of war under King Jesus? _____

We don't take Michael's place, but are we expected to fight alongside him? Explain please.

In your own words list from Ephesians 6 what it means to be a warrior alongside Michael and under the authority of Jesus Christ as our Warrior of Peace.

Tell me in your own words what defensive and offensive weapons have already been given to you.

Do you feel you are using these weapons properly?

Are you willing to put in the time it takes to be a prepared warrior for this last battle with Jesus Christ?

Please write your commitment to Him as your Commander and Chief.

Chapter Fourteen
How To Be Led by the Holy Spirit

After these studies on the Holy Spirit, you may feel like you are already being led by the Holy Spirit. You probably are being led to some degree. I want you to feel confident that in all seasons and situations you are hearing from the Holy Spirit at all times. He doesn't come and go, and you shouldn't either. He moves into your being and never leaves you. The Holy Spirit is for you! He has been given to the earth by Father God to help you succeed in every area of your life for the rest of your life!

Ultimately, Father God wants you to be reunited with Him forever as His own child. Romans 8:14 states _____
_____

What is your greatest assurance from that verse?
_____
_____
_____
_____

What are you supposed to do when you fail?
_____
_____
_____
_____

Who advocates for us in the court of heaven?
_____
_____
_____
_____

Can you wrap your mind around the fact that two members of the Godhead advocate for you in a legal heavenly court system before the Righteous Judge who only wants you to win and never wants you to lose? Explain your feelings.
_____
_____
_____
_____
_____

Having the Holy Spirit with us is like Jesus being with the disciples in the flesh. Do we treat the Holy Spirit with the same devotion that the disciples treated Jesus? They left everything to follow Him? Have you left everything to be with the Holy Spirit for the rest of your life? Explain. What have you left behind to be assured of your being called a child of the living God?

_____
_____
_____
_____
_____
_____
_____

Jesus told the disciples in John 15:8 what they were required to do to show themselves to be true followers of Him. How can you relate this to your own life and walk with the Holy Spirit as Jesus' representative today?

_____
_____
_____
_____
_____
_____

Do you keep His commandments? _____

Do you obey His orders and follow His plan? _____

Do you abide in Him always? _____

All these answers prove that you understand and are walking in 1 John 3:24. If you can't answer these questions, fully knowing and understanding that He is in you and that you are in Him, then this would be a good time to stop and repent before Almighty God. Start again with your relationship with Him if need be. Write what you are feeling.

_____
_____
_____
_____
_____
_____
_____
_____

When we are led by the Holy Spirit, we are filled with His _____.

As we stand before the Righteous Judge, we need evidence to prove we are who we say we are. What life evidence do we have that proves our lip service to our God?

_____
_____
_____
_____
_____
_____

Giving up the need to be in control is a sign that you have _____
_____
_____

The Holy Spirit won't fight you for the lead. If you want the lead, He will let you have it. Explain here where you have struggled in this area of your life and what you are willing to do differently?

_____
_____
_____
_____
_____
_____

According to 2 Corinthians 6:17-18, what is required of us to prove the Holy Spirit has full control of our lives?

_____
_____
_____
_____

Do you love Him? Explain.

_____
_____
_____
_____
_____

Do you trust Him? Explain.

Chapter Fifteen
The Seven-Fold Spirits of God

Write out these scripture references to the seven Spirits of God.

Revelation 3:1

Revelation 4:5

Revelation 5:6

Sometimes I can't see things plainly until I write them out. I want you to see through your own handwriting the multifaceted persona of the Holy Spirit through the scriptures.

Who have you allowed the Holy Spirit to be in your life so far?

Who does He need to be to help you go further in your walk and calling?

The Holy Spirit is on duty all over the earth according to Revelation 5:6. How does that make you feel?

_____
_____
_____
_____

The Holy Spirit speaks through humanity. Are you willing to allow Him to speak through you? When was the last time you allowed Him to speak through you? Explain.

_____
_____
_____
_____
_____
_____
_____
_____

List the seven-fold Spirits of God.
1. _____
2. _____
3. _____
4. _____
5. _____
6. _____
7. _____

Why is Holy the first one?

_____
_____
_____
_____
_____

The first level of who we are is explained in our name. The same goes for the Holy Spirit. His first and foremost persona is in His name, Holy Spirit.

Explain the benefit of housing the Holy Spirit in your being and what it means to you personally to be holy.

_____

To be one with the Holy Spirit, we must house His seven-fold Spirits and become one with all seven Spirits. Explain each one in detail regarding how they operate within your life.

Holy Spirit

_____

Wisdom Spirit

_____

Understanding Spirit

_____

Counsel Spirit

_____
_____
_____
_____

Might Spirit

_____
_____
_____
_____
_____
_____

Knowledge Spirit

_____
_____
_____
_____
_____

Fear of the Lord Spirit

_____
_____
_____
_____
_____

Each one is personal to you. Each one can save you in different moments in your life. If you would like to write a letter of thanks to the seven-fold Spirits of God, I will give you space to do so here.

_____
_____
_____
_____
_____

You are a container for the Holy Spirit to fill. Jesus received all of the Holy Spirit within Him and so must you. Jesus prayed a prayer to Father God in John 17, and I am asking you to write your own personal prayer to the Father here concerning your infilling and surrender to the Holy Spirit. Please write your prayer as you pray it to Father God.

_____
_____
_____
_____
_____
_____
_____
_____
_____
_____
_____
_____
_____
_____
_____

When you become the center of the cross, so to speak, in your heavenly/earthly life walk, your relationship with the Holy Spirit (heavenly) will give you the power to have earthly relationships based upon the Godhead within you. Learning to practice His presence daily and operate your life's journey based upon the leading of the Holy Spirit is a wonderful way to live your life in the peace of God. After reading this book and working this workbook, can you see a place to improve your own daily walk with others?

_____
_____
_____

We have gifts from heaven through the Holy Spirit living within us. Have you chosen to receive all of these nine gifts? Explain how each gift can and will operate through you daily if you give Him a place to do so.

_____
_____
_____
_____
_____

When you receive the Holy Spirit, you have the opportunity to fruit nine separate manifestations each day in your relationships with others. Explain how these nine fruit levels can change your daily life while walking with others.

When you receive the Holy Spirit, you receive His power not only within you but also covering you. Luke 24:49 speaks of this covering as being clothed from on high with power. Explain how you experience this and can experience this every day of your life with others.

Chapter Sixteen
Holy Spirit Is Our Witness in Heaven and Earth

Did you realize before reading this chapter that the Holy Spirit is always with you and always witnessing in the legal court of heaven for or against you? He must give an account of what He experiences by being with you constantly. Are you giving the Holy Spirit what He needs to witness for you in the court of heaven?

_____
_____
_____

Acts 5:32 states that the Holy Spirit is bestowed on those who obey Him. We must realize that if a person seems to "not be able" to receive the Holy Spirit, it could be because Father God loves that person so much. What could I mean by that? Father God knows everything about us including our future. When He knows that in our future we won't obey the Holy Spirit, then He doesn't give the Holy Spirit to the one who won't obey Him! I believe it would be much worse for us to have the Holy Spirit and not obey Him than not to have the Holy Spirit! Remember the consequence for quenching the Holy Spirit and blaspheming the Holy Spirit.

Write the two scripture references to those two statements.
1. Quenching the Holy Spirit _____

2. Blaspheming the Holy Spirit _____

Can you see how much the Father must love us to withhold the Holy Spirit from the person He knows will quench and/or blaspheme the Holy Spirit? Oh, the love of God for us to protect us from what He knows that we can't possibly know! Write your thoughts here. Would you like to stop for a moment and repent? Feel free to do so. I have stopped my writing many times to drop to my knees and ask Father to forgive me when I have delayed my obedience (which is disobedience).

_____
_____
_____
_____
_____
_____
_____
_____
_____
_____

There are three witnesses in heaven.
1. _____
2. _____
3. _____

Are the three heaven witnesses witnessing for you or against you? Explain why.
_____
_____
_____
_____
_____
_____
_____

There are three witnesses in earth.
1. _____
2. _____
3. _____

Explain how these witnesses bring us victory.
_____
_____
_____
_____
_____
_____
_____
_____

Ephesians 5:26 explains how we can be clean and stay clean. Write it out and explain how it works in your personal life.
_____
_____
_____
_____
_____
_____
_____

How can the blood of Jesus witness for me in the court of heaven? Explain.

Before we had the three witnesses for us, Father God had to call heaven and earth to witness. Each witness mentioned in scripture is a witness against us. Give those three references and write them out.

1.

2.

3.

Explain why it was that way in the Old Testament.

Why is it different now for us?

How important is it that we guard our words and our hearts?

How can we get our tongues in a position where they speak differently?

Until we learn to control our tongues by the Holy Spirit, we should exercise our right to remain _____ (like Zacharias in Luke 1).

When we become one with Jesus Christ through the Holy Spirit, who witnesses for us? Who puts in a word for us?

We should never plead our own case before the Righteous Judge. We should simply _____.

We can change a whole nation with our surrendering prayer much like Solomon in 2 Chronicles 7:1-3. Write your prayer for our nation and ask without reservation for what will bring change instead of what will make us comfortable.

_____
_____
_____
_____
_____
_____
_____
_____
_____
_____
_____
_____

Father, take not Your Holy Spirit from me. Would you like to pray this prayer also? Use your own words to express your heart to the Father about the Holy Spirit.

_____
_____
_____
_____
_____
_____
_____
_____

The Bible uses many metaphors to describe the Holy Spirit. Describe the Holy Spirit in your life.

_____
_____
_____
_____
_____
_____
_____
_____

Now that you have walked this journey with me, would you close this workbook with a prayer of praise and thanksgiving to Father God for the Holy Spirit and His power within you? If it comes out as a song, that's even better! Write it below after you have prayed in the Holy Spirit prayer language for awhile.

_____
_____
_____
_____
_____
_____
_____
_____
_____
_____
_____
_____
_____
_____
_____
_____
_____
_____
_____
_____
_____
_____
_____
_____
_____
_____
_____
_____
_____

Get comfortable praying in tongues and never stop again. This is the best and easiest way to pray without ceasing!

Now write the interpretation.

Thank you for staying with me and finishing what you have started. This shows that you have the Holy Spirit's character developing in you. The Holy Spirit is a finisher. He never quits or walks away. He is the Spirit of a finisher. When you have finished this workbook, please email me at my personal email (cheryl@salemfamilyministries.org) and tell me what you think of this journey.

If you have enjoyed this book and workbook, please write a review on Amazon and give me five stars!

Don't forget to join me weekly on our Salem Family Ministries YouTube channel. Let's continue to study the Word of God together and pray in the Holy Spirit! I will see you there!

About the Author

Cheryl Salem walked the runway to become Miss America 1980, despite what appeared to be all odds stacked against her. A horrific car crash resulting in a physical handicap and over 100 stitches in her face, were no match for what God had planned for her life. Through childlike faith in Him, she overcame the obstacles and eventually took the crown in Atlantic City to become Miss America 1980. She has used this distinction as a springboard to launch the gospel into churches, women's conferences, and many television appearances. According to Cheryl, "None of these things would be possible, if not for my Jesus."

In 1985, Cheryl married the love of her life, Harry Salem II. Harry and Cheryl Salem travel the world ministering the gospel, telling people that Jesus loves them and that He is returning soon! Their lives revolve around seeking the Lord and where He would have them go. Two by two they travel, loving God's people, living and moving in His anointing.

In 1999, Harry and Cheryl endured the loss of their 6-year-old daughter, Gabrielle. As they boldly took steps of faith to overcome the agonizing pain of Gabrielle's death, they asked God to restore them and for souls to come into His kingdom. God has restored the Salem family and because of His mighty anointing, the altars have been full!

Harry and Cheryl are committed to leading godly lives as an example to their sons, Harry III and Roman. In 2012 Roman married a beautiful young lady, Stephanie, and she became their daughter-in-love. Healing and restoration came full circle to the Salem family with the miracle births of Roman and Stephanie's children, Mia Gabrielle and Roman Harry.

Cheryl and Harry have written over forty books. From her first book to her last, Cheryl's books are open and honest with such transparency you can almost hear her talking to you while you read! She has recorded numerous worship music projects, from prophetic books of the Bible, lullabies, instrumentals, prophetic flowing intercession, and beautiful worship CDs.

Harry and Cheryl are walking out the Lord's plan in their sessions of *School of Worship*. These are intensive training schools where the Salems teach, impart, and personally work with students to help them grow to the next level in their worship, life, and ministry.

Cheryl is founder and president of Women Of The Nation, an organization that is bringing together thousands of women who stand, pray and believe for this country. Under Cheryl's leadership these women are strategic, organized, unified and in prayer for our great nation. God gave Cheryl authority when she was crowned Miss America, and she is using that authority to stand in the gap for this great nation, for such a time as this!

Other books by Salem Family Ministries

**Holy Spirit*

Quips, Quotes, and Wisdom Notes

*Three Stages of Life

*Women of the Nation Pray!

*I Am A Worshiper

*I Am A Worshiper Workbook

*We Who Worship

*We Who Worship Workbook

*Rebuilding the Ruins of Worship

*Rebuilding the Ruins of Worship Workbook

*Tones of the Throne Room

*Tones of the Throne Room Workbook

*The Rise of an Orphan Generation: Longing for a Father

*Two Becoming One

*Don't Kill Each Other! Let God Do It!

*From Mourning to Morning

*From Grief to Glory

Distractions from Destiny

*Obtaining Peace - A 40-Day Prayer Journal

*Entering Rest - Be Still A 40-Day Prayer Journey

The Presence of Angels in Your Life

Overcoming Fear – A 40-Day Prayer Journal

*A Bright Shining Place - The Story of a Miracle

Speak the Word Over Your Family for Healing

Speak the Word Over Your Family for Finances

Speak the Word Over Your Family for Salvation

A Royal Child

The Mommy Book

Abuse . . . Bruised but not Broken

You Are Somebody

Choose to be Happy (out of print)

Health and Beauty Secrets (out of print)

Simple Facts: Salvation, Healing & the Holy Ghost (out of print)

Every Body Needs Balance (out of print)

The Choice is Yours (out of print)

Being #1 at Being #2 (out of print)

For Men Only (out of print)

It's Too Soon to Give Up (out of print)

Covenant Conquerors (out of print)

Warriors of the Word (out of print)

Fight in the Heavenlies (out of print)

Written by Dr. Harry Salem III

*Grave Raiders

*Feminine Spirits and Angels

*Investigating Wonders

*The Sound of the Spirit

*Age of Mystery

*Counting Ten Fingers for Patience Children's Book

*Ten Shots for Do and Don't Children's Book

*Ten Steps to Build and Be Spirit Filled Children's Book

*Count of Ten Say Amen Children's Book

*EBooks available at salemfamilyministries.org

Worship CDs and downloads are also available

If you would like more information about Salem Family Ministries, you can write to us or contact us via email on our website.

Salem Family Ministries

P. O. Box 1595

Cathedral City, CA 92235

www.salemfamilyministries.org

https://www.facebook.com/salemfamilyministries.org/

Subscribe to our YouTube channel Salem Family Ministries

Follow me on Instagram, CherylSalem1957

Made in the USA
Middletown, DE
04 February 2025